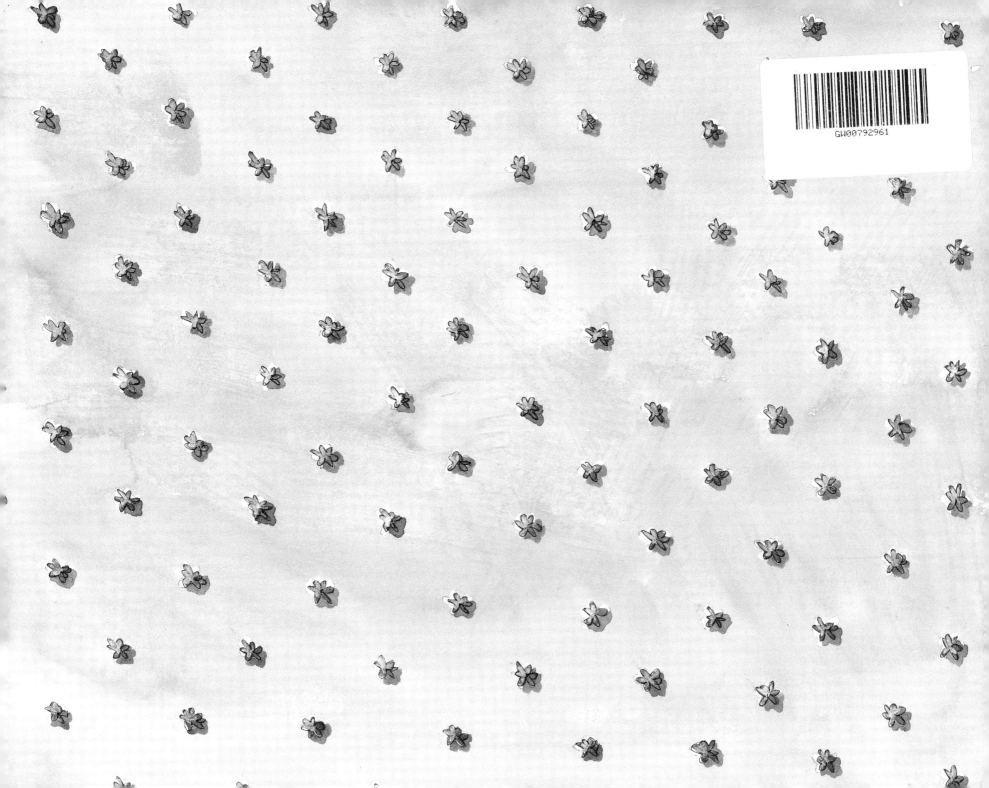

GW00792961

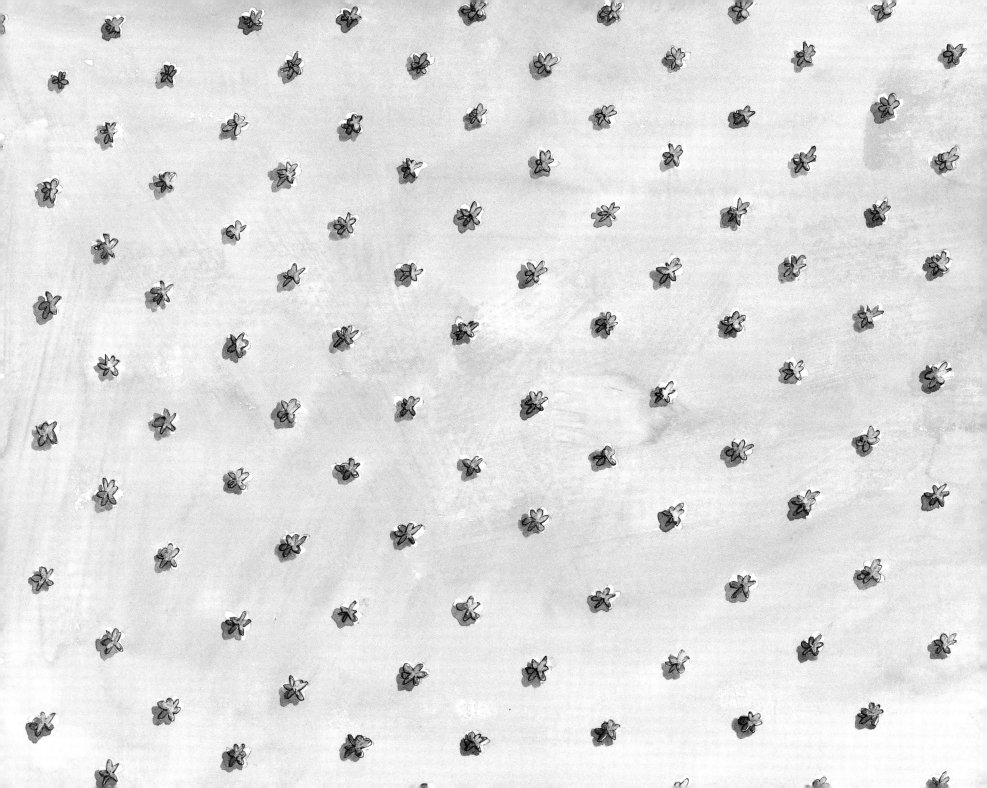

For Christine, Pearse and Seamus - M.D.

For Ruby - M. de B.

RED SAILS MARKETING

21 West Avenue, Portstewart, BT55 7NB
www.redsailsmarketing.com

This paperback edition was first published in 2005

50p from every copy sold will be donated to
Habitat for Humanity Northern Ireland (HFHNI), a cross-community,
Christian self-build housing organisation which helps low-income families
build and purchase their own homes at a price they can afford.
www.habitatni.co.uk

**Habitat for Humanity®
Northern Ireland**

ISBN 0-9549953-0-9

Printed By Easyprint, Belfast

Every time you see a bee, you might think of Barnaby

For he's the bee who makes the honey

That is so good and tastes so Yummy

He lives on a farm with all his friends
Where the fun and laughter never ends.

They all help to make the honey
That makes the day so bright and sunny.

Every day and every hour they buzz around from flower to flower,

To get the nectar so clear and runny.that's used to make some lovely honey

The busy bees inside the hive
Work hard all day, they toil and strive

To use the nectar to make the honey
It's now gooey and sweet and really yummy.

Then Farmer Hugh puts it in pots and sells it in his market shop.

The taste and goodness of lovely honey
"Quick, go and get some mummy!"

Yippee

It's honey for tea!

Thanks to you little Barnaby.

For I love the taste of golden honey, especially when it's....

...inside my tummy!

The End

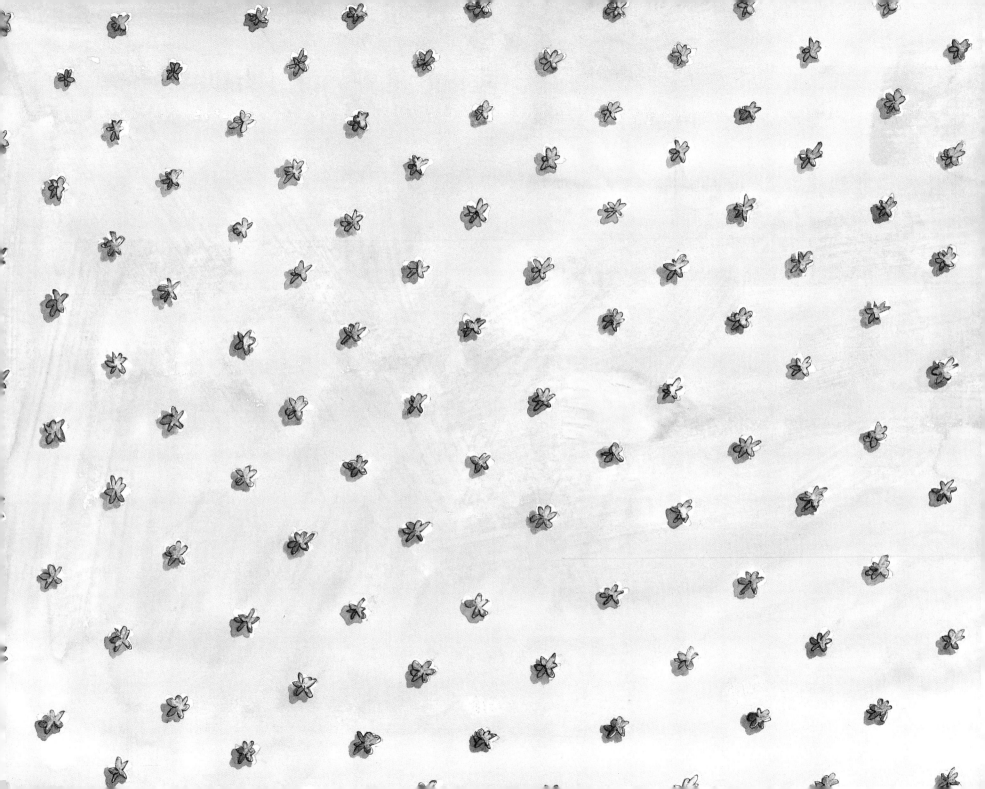